Kateri's Monster Tales: Based on Haudenosaunee Folktales

Cathy Smith

Published by Cathy Smith, 2019.

KATERI'S MONSTER TALES: BASED ON HAUDENOSAUNEE FOLKTALES

First edition. February 23, 2019.

Copyright © 2019 Cathy Smith.

ISBN: 979-8230936114

Written by Cathy Smith.

Table of Contents

Jitkwa:e vs the Snakes

PATRICK BURNING'S VISITS to his grandfather, Totah, was a duty to both his family and his culture. Mom would've stayed in the Bush if she didn't need to leave it to find work. Every summer he went to Totah's place to learn about his people's traditions. Now she wanted him to get an Indian name at the Green Corn Ceremony.

Going back to the Bush was like visiting a parallel universe. One that could turn hostile if you offended an obscure custom you were unaware of. He found this out when he once said Seneca was his "tribe", instead of his "nation." He still said "tribe" among his non-native friends and had to say "nation" on the Rez.

If his family cared about his name so much why did they put "Patrick Burning" on his birth certificate 15 years ago? Maybe he should let the Faith Keepers give him whatever name they wanted? He feared that the Indian name would have a dorky English translation. Maybe they'd take suggestions? So, he googled possible Seneca names for himself.

His conversation about it with Totah hadn't been encouraging. "It will be in our native tongue and have a special meaning."

"Oh—well I hope it'll have a cool meaning then. Maybe Othagwenda? It has a meaning that's cool and easy to remember, 'Flint.'"

"You will NOT be named 'Othagwenda '." Totah grimaced.

Patrick's brows came together when he saw Totah frown. "What's wrong with 'Othagwenda '?"

"One of the Bad Twin's names is 'Othagwenda '. He's not as bad as the white man's Devil, but he's not someone I want you named after. You won't be 'Othagwenda,'"

Another Google search brought vocabulary lists of Seneca words. Nothing caught his eye. In his desperation he clicked one search result about "The Battle of the Snakes: A Seneca Legend.":

Jitkwa:e hated snakes so much that he'd burn any snake he found alive and tortured them to death.

The snakes became so angry they convened a war council and declared a war on Jitkwa:e's village. When they swarmed the village. The villagers built a fire along their barricades to scare them away. The snakes slithered over the fire. Snakes at the bottom of the pyre died, but smothered the fire. The living snakes were so intent on the battle they crawled over their fallen brothers.

The poisonous vipers found and converged on Jitkwa: e and bit him to death. He died howling in agony as the poisons ate through his body.

His screams pleased the Chief of the Snakes. He felt so generous he offered to end the hostilities with the villagers. However, they had to agree to never name a man in their tribe "Jitkwa:e" again.

The village agreed to the terms of this treaty, and that's why the name "Jitkwa:e" is forbidden among the Seneca.

Patrick gasped. He found his Indian name! He texted it to all of his friends and changed all of his online avatars to read Jitkwa:e with his mobile apps.

It put him in such a good mood he didn't mind it when Totah made him work in the garden that afternoon. This time half the garden had mounds. "I found an article about traditional Haudenosaunee gardening. I'm trying the old methods this year for the corns, beans and squash," Totah said.

The rest of the vegetable garden was in regular rows. There were plump tomatoes. They smelled like they were already cooked in spices like a well-made tomato sauce. They made Patrick's mouth water.

"Pick some for BLT sandwiches tonight," Totah said.

A vine moved while Patrick picked some ripe tomatoes. When it continued moving, he got a queasy feeling in his stomach when he realized it wasn't a vine. He started when a snake slithered over his rubber boots.

"Aaahh!" Patrick shook the snake off his boot and kicked it out of the garden. It hissed at him. Totah stepped in front of it with a rake.

The snake coiled as if it would launch itself at Patrick despite Totah's upraised rake. The sound of thunder in the distance made it hiss instead. It cast a glance at Patrick and crawled away.

Totah shook his head. "It was a milk snake! They're poisonous!"

Droplets of rain fell, and the rumbling grew louder. "We better get inside before the storm gets worse," Totah said.

He griped on his profiles about his day and got an immediate response on his wall, *Bummer, man! If snakes don't scare you what about a bush bash?*

The question came from Wyrm Ware who had an avatar with a piece of closeup beadwork. Patrick assumed he must be from the Rez.

I'm not in the mood for a powwow.

A bush bash isn't a powwow.

What's the diff?

A bush bash is at night.

Patrick chuckled at this.

He was referred to a "Where You At" app to guide him there. Patrick set the alarm on his smartphone to wake him up...

When it was time to head out the Where You Are app showed where he had to go. He only needed to grab his jacket, shoes and house key before he headed out.

Totah had never set a curfew because Patrick went to bed early, anyway. He pretended to turn in, so he could text his friends on his smartphone. He turned off the lights so that Totah would assume he was asleep. However, he stayed awake in bed until ten to eleven p.m. This was the first time he'd heard of an after dark party!

He took his stuff and crept out as soundlessly as he could. The wooden floorboards let out a creak on a noisy step. He stopped, his heart pounded, but there was nothing. Either Totah was asleep or assumed he'd been struck by the midnight munchies. He walked out as lightly as possible and walked out of the front door and locked it.

There was a full moon that night and the app also acted as a flashlight and an interactive map once he was outside. The app showed him a path in the woods outside Totah's house. He grimaced when his feet squished on some mud, *Who'll want to party in this?*

He jumped when he heard loud footsteps, and turned to face a boy his age, if boys his age seriously worked out. Unless he was a lacrosse athlete? The boy was half a head shorter than him and had dark eyes, and long glossy black hair. He also had a smartphone. Patrick assumed he was invited to the bush bash too. He walked straight up to Patrick and said in a deep voice, "Are you Jitkwa:e?"

"Hmm?" Patrick asked.

"Are you Jitkwa:e?" he held up a smartphone that had the post on Patrick's wall.

"Yeah, that's me," Patrick said.

The boy gave a snort, "I wouldn't brag about it if I were you."

"Huh?" Patrick frowned.

"I wouldn't brag about being yellow," the boy said.

"Who said I'm yellow?" Patrick said.

The boy smirked, as he called up the comments to the post. "Buck! Buck!" A streaming video of a baby chick with yellow fuzz was embedded in the post. He chuckled at this.

"Humph, you never know what will set things off in the Bush," Patrick snorted.

"Why are you out here if you can't get along with anyone?" the boy asked.

Patrick drew himself up to his full height, "I don't get cyberbullied by everyone here. I got invited to a bush bash."

"Are you so sure of that? The only thing you'll find out here is snakes."

"You sound like my Totah. He won't let me do anything our ancestors wouldn't have done in Pre–Contact days!"

The boy frowned and there was a far-off rumble.

"Oh, "Patrick groaned. He would have to skip the Bush Party. He headed back to Totah's without bothering to say "bye" to the boy. By the time he got back it was raining, and thunder flashed when he entered the house and closed the door.

His smartphone kept vibrating as he walked up to the guest bedroom. He assumed that it was Wyrm Ware, checking to see where he was. *They must really be party animals if they want to be out in this storm*!

When he looked down at it he saw that there was a writhing snake wallpaper on the screen he couldn't get rid of. He had a virus!

PATRICK TALKED TO TOTAH at breakfast the next morning. "When I checked my mobile, I found this on my screen." He gestured to the writhing viper screen-saver he couldn't get rid of. "I must have a virus. Is there an IT person here I can talk to?"

"There's an outlet on the reserve," Totah said. "We can have him look at your phone."

Patrick wanted to go as soon as the shop opened. Totah would drive him over. He stepped out of the house to find a garter snake at the doorstep.

The scent of this fear emboldened the snake, and it hissed at him.

The garter snake launched itself at Patrick like a rattlesnake. Totah shoved Patrick aside and kicked the creature out of the way with his high boots. It fell back ten feet, and made as if to crawl forward. Then there was a flash of light in the distance from a far-off thundercloud. The snake gave one last hiss before slithering away.

Totah shook his head, "I've never seen a garter snake act like that. Most times they're scared of people. You'd think it had something personal against you."

TOTAH COOKED EXTRA slices of bacon for the BLT sandwiches that night. He poured the resultant grease into a glass jar. "Snakes don't like the smell of pigs' fat. Let's see if it keeps them away."

The next day they headed out to the computer store again. When there were no snakes waiting for them Patrick let out a whoop.

Thunder boomed and rain fell as soon as Patrick stepped outside the front door, "Oh!"

"We'll wait until it passes," Totah said.

"It's not fair! I won't be able to talk to my friends until I get this malware off my smartphone," Patrick groaned.

Fifteen minutes later the sky cleared, "Let's try it."

"Patrick."

A loud boom shook the foundations of the house. "What's with all this freak weather?"

"Maybe it's that climate change everyone is talking about," Totah sighed.

"ALL THESE THUNDERSTORMS are making the Faithkeepers nervous. They think they should schedule a ceremony for the Thunderers. They've all been burning tobacco whenever there is a lightning strike, but it doesn't seem to work. This weird weather is scaring them."

Patrick wondered if the storms were because of climate change. Shouldn't climate change frighten the Old Timers more than angry Thunderers?

"I've called a fortuneteller to come to us," Totah continued.

"A fortuneteller?" Patrick asked.

"We need to find out why you're having this run of bad luck. It could be a bad omen," Totah said. He phoned a friend of his, took out money and a packet of Indian Tobacco.

There were no snakes at the front door. The bacon grease did the trick and repelled them. An old lady knocked at the door an hour later. She introduced herself as Elma Henhawk. Patrick didn't know what to expect from her. He was surprised when she made them loose-leaf tea after she entered Totah's house.

"So, what do you do? Read my palm?" Patrick asked as he took a sip.

"Finish your tea," Elma said.

When he finished drinking, she studied the fall of the leaves in the cup. The leaves fell into a long winding line crossed with a long-jagged line.

"So you're the one that calls himself 'Jitkwa:e' online!"

Patrick blinked. "You can tell that from the tea leaves?"

"Me and most of the Bush have profiles online, but I can read tea leaves too. The leaves are telling me the snakes are mad at you for taking on the forbidden name. And it's no wonder the Thunderers are so worked up." Elma pointed to the winding and the jagged lines created by the tea leaves.

"Do the Thunderers want to throw thunderbolts at me too?" Patrick asked.

"It's a part of the Thunderer's job to protect the Onkwehon:we from the Serpents," Elma said. "They must be holding the snakes back from their planned war."

Totah grimaced. "We need to call the Faithkeepers and tell them to give Patrick his new name, now!".

"I don't like snakes, but if they leave me alone, I'll be happy to leave them alone," Patrick said.

"You're using 'Jitkwa:e' online is an insult to all snakes everywhere. The natural and supernatural snakes are angry, Patrick," Elma said. "You're putting yourself, and everyone at the Bush in danger by keeping that name. You don't want to die being 'yellow.'"

"Why are you calling me 'yellow?' Using a forbidden name isn't yellow," Patrick sniffed.

"It's bad enough to disrespect the snakes. You're also disrespecting our people's traditions," Totah said.

"Totah!" Patrick rolled his eyes.

"We'll let you be yellow if you want to be stubborn," Elma said.

"Why do you keep saying I'm yellow?"

"That's what 'Jitkwa:e' means in Seneca," Elma said.

Patrick groaned. The Thunderers, snakes, and villagers would get what they wanted from him. It wasn't worth getting everyone mad at him over a lame name!

AN EMERGENCY MEETING of the Longhouse was held at Totah's the next day. They wanted to give Patrick a new Indian name. Erma made some lyed corn soup, scones, roasted ham, an apple pie and strawberry infused water for the event. Totah wasn't able to go out shopping, so he gave her money to cover the cost of supplies.

Patrick considered himself lucky his people's weather gods didn't want blood. Tobacco was the cure all for their spirit beings. Totah didn't smoke, but had plenty of loose-leaf tobacco on hand for the event.

He made Patrick wear the black slacks, and ribbon shirt he'd picked out for the event. At least the shirt fabric wasn't calico. He respected most of his people's traditions, but didn't want to wear flowery fabric. His ribbon shirt was of a solid red fabric. It had white and black ribbons sewn on flat at the bottom of the bodice. The ends of the ribbons were left long and hanging on either side of him. He was glad it wasn't the fashion to tie them up in bows.

Totah and Patrick greeted all the people who came in. Erma carried in the food from her car and handed it to them once she crossed their threshold. They would've gone to the car to help her but couldn't risk another run in with snakes and freak storms.

Patrick looked forward to a hot meal even if the ceremony didn't work. Almost all the Faith Keepers were older than Patrick. He recognized the one called Beau Striker as the boy he'd seen the last time he was out of the house. He assumed Beau was an immersion kid who knew the language and ceremonies.

Patrick smirked at the sight of Beau's blue-grey eyes when he got a look at him in better lighting. You would've thought he was a full blood the way he lectured about their people's customs that night.

The Fire Keeper, Ernest Smoke, had wispy white hair and wore a gustowe headdress. Every male in the party wore a ribbon shirt and pants set.

Erma was the only woman there. She wore a long purple calico dress that reached to her calves, with black leggings that had beaded hems. She set up the food while Ernest set up the fire in the fireplace.

Leon Skye was a man in his mid–thirties. He chanted the Thanksgiving Address in their original language. The only words Patrick could make out was "Our Grandfathers the Thunderers…"

He didn't know when the ritual ended until Totah said, "Your name is now Ni:io."

"It means nothing embarrassing?" Patrick asked.

"It means 'all is well,'" Leon said in English.

Beau nodded at this, "Grandfather will be pleased." His eyes were now a bright blue. There was a rumble and a flash of light that blinded everyone.

"It didn't work!" Patrick gasped during the moment of blindness.

When their sight returned Beau was gone.

"Humph?" Totah muttered.

The sky was the color of Beau's eyes. He glanced at Erma, "Beau's gone back to his grandfather."

Totah's eyes widened, but Patrick didn't know what it meant.

Patrick's smartphone chimed. He glanced at it. There was no Wyrm Ware screen-saver, so he could see the dozens of texts from his friends he had to catch up on…

The Hand

JASON MARTIN THOUGHT it was so unfair that people didn't get the day off to celebrate Halloween. At least Halloween was on a Saturday this year, so he got to sleep over at his friend, Alan Henry's, house on Friday night. He helped Allan decorate his house. The two kept taking snapshots of every piece of their chosen Halloween decorations. They posted them on Instagram. The pieces that got the most votes were set off to be placed outside. Others were tweaked and reposted on Instagram. When they got a decent number of votes, they were ready to put them out to the public.

Jason groaned when he saw that his latest piece got no votes. It was a monster hand glove stuffed to look like a severed hand.

Allan took one look at it spread out on the kitchen table. "You might get more likes if you use a full dummy to make it look like a corpse."

"It's supposed to be 'the Hand.'"

Allan sniffed, "I think a full zombie would be scarier!"

"I don't care what Instagram says: a hand was good enough for our ancestors. It's good enough for me," Jason said.

Allan's eyes drifted upward, but he stopped himself from doing a full eye-roll. His family had only moved back to the Rez two years ago. He didn't know enough about their people's traditions to come up with a good comeback.

They moved on from the decorations to put finishing touches on their costumes. Jason put fake blood on his plastic knife and brown coveralls. Allan had a screaming ghost mask with a matching black outfit. The outfit was too small to fit him, so he found black jeans and a black hoodie he could use. "I oughtta sue! The only thing I can use from the costume I bought is the mask!"

"Maybe our moms will let us see the movies these costumes come from in a year or two," Jason sighed. His own mom was a big believer in the movie rating system, and wouldn't let him see anything over a PG-13. He looked forward to the day when he could stream "The Walking Dead."

"We won't have anything else to post until we go trick or treating tomorrow," Jason said.

Allan checked his feed on his smartphone. He saw a #BloodyMary hashtag, "There's a Bloody Mary challenge tonight."

He showed Jason pictures of kids with scratched faces, arms, and backs.

Jason looked it over, "It looks like they've been cutting themselves. There's no way Bloody Mary could scratch all those people at once."

Allan grimaced at the sight of one girl with a deep cut on her arm. "I don't think anyone should do this to themselves for a trending challenge."

Jason shrugged, "Some people will do anything for a like."

"I'd like to try it."

"Try what? Scratching yourself?" Jason sniffed.

"Not myself. I'd like to see if Bloody Mary would do it for me."

"Bloody Mary is a white man's ghost! We're more likely to see the Hand on the Rez. It doesn't like to see Indian kids out after dark. It'll smack you around if it catches you outside," Jason said as he slammed his palms together.

"Who told you that?" Allan asked.

Jason said, "Totah. "

"Totah?" Allan asked.

"Totah's my grandpa. Though you can call any elder that," Jason said.

"Maybe he said that to make you keep your curfew?" Allan asked. "It'd never work with my big bro, Gary. He didn't wait until he was 18 to go out past midnight. All Mom could do was stop waiting up for him after his birthday two months ago."

"We'll see if you're right when we camp out tonight. I'll put up with a slap if I can get a picture." Jason held up his smartphone camera with those words.

"That's so lame! I don't need a Hand to get slapped around. All I need to do is get on Gary's bad side, " Allan said with a laugh. "Our ancestors must've been wimps if they were so easy to scare in the old days."

"Well they had the Okiiweh, the Feast of the Dead, which is creepier than the white man's Halloween," Jason said.

"Feast of the Dead, "Allan mused, "It sounds like it'd be cool, what happens?"

"Every 12 years our ancestors would dig up the graves of the people who'd died since the last feast. They put their bones in a mass grave after a ceremony was held." Jason said.

"What if they died in the past few months and weren't bony yet?" Allan asked.

"Then their bones would be cleaned up and placed in the mass grave. "Jason wanted to give more details but Allan's EEEWWW! stopped him.

"Give me a holiday that gives me a candy not a gross out!" Allan sniffed.

"It's not much worse than what goes on in a funeral home nowadays. "

"Maybe, but I wouldn't want to hear how they do their work either. 'Sides that who wants go through crying over burying someone twice? Longhouse people don't still do that do they?" Allan shivered.

"No, they just clean the graves, have a ceremony, and burn tobacco," Jason said.

Allan chuckled. "The Longhouse People are probably too scared of the Health Department to do more than that..."

Once they settled on their costumes Jason posed over a helpless pumpkin. He loomed over it with a large carving knife in his Hockey Mask Killer costume. Allan streamed a video of him chanting, "Die! Die! Die!" as he kept plunging the knife into the pumpkin's flesh.

Gary called out to them off–camera and said. "Turn that off!"

Allan frowned, "Huh?"

"I need to get stuff from the kitchen. I don't want you tagging my Halloween costume online," Gary said.

"Oh," Allan turned his smartphone camera off, and Gary came in with a knapsack. His face was painted white, so he looked pasty and there were black patches on his eyes. Strategic blotches of red on his face made it look like he was bleeding. He took out two cartons of eggs from the fridge. He placed the cartons in the bag. The boys also noticed the spray cans, toilet paper rolls and self-defense baton already inside it. "What are you doing?" Allan asked, "Mom will be mad at you if you waste so many groceries."

"Tonight's Devil's Night. I'm going out." Gary said.

"Can we go with you?" Allan asked.

"Yeah, it'd give us something cool to post on Instagram," Jason said.

"You don't livestream yourself with your public account on Devil's Night! That be as stupid as posting on Facebook Live while you're knocking over a store," Gary sputtered.

"It wouldn't be worth going along with you if we can't share it on Instagram," Allan sighed.

Gary snorted, "Stupid."

"Maybe we're better off staying home? The Hand doesn't like Indian kids to go out after dark," Jason said.

"What about all those lacrosse games I see kids go to? They start during the day and end at night in the evenings," Gary said.

"Maybe he's a fan? Or the lacrosse may act as a medicine. It's the Creator's game," Jason shrugged.

"What can a hand do to you, anyway?" Gary sniffed.

"It'll slap you silly."

Gary shook his head, "Weird! What kind of wussy ghost slaps people around? That might've been scary back in the old days, but it doesn't cut it today!"

Allan said, "See, I was right, Jason. You need a full zombie to scare people nowadays."

"Well if you two can't handle a full zombie, then I better leave you at home," Gary walked out of the kitchen with those words.

"Oh!" Jason sputtered.

"We've still got the backyard tonight," Allan said.

THEY PUT OUT THE HALLOWEEN decorations in the front yard. Then they set up their tent and supplies in the backyard before it got dark. Allan's mom watched Allan more closely than Gary. She made them put out extra blankets, sleeping bags, and flash lights in the tent.

"Let's get Bloody Mary over with and then we'll wait for the Hand." Allan said.

They went inside to use the bathroom for the challenge, and had to plan it out first. "OK have the smartphones ready to take videos of Bloody Mary."

"I don't think they'll pick anything up in a dark room."

"I got an old nightlight. We'll plug it into the outlet to see if it works and see what kind of pictures the smartphone takes in the lighting."

Jason snickered when a teddy bear nightlight was produced. "Are you sure she'll want to show up with that thing around?"

"It's all I've got."

The nightlight was plugged into a bathroom outlet. The teddy bear gave off a comfortable glow in the dark. Jason held up his smartphone and took a picture of Allan next to the nightlight, "Hey!"

"I had to make sure you showed up in the pic."

"Humph, you better not post that on Instagram," Allan said.

"I'll only do it if it becomes a "before" picture."

Allan scrunched his nose. "Let's take the before picture in the hallway away from the teddy bear nightlight."

They went into the hallway and posed for selfies to use as their before pictures.

"Let's forget the video and take selfies in the hallway when we get out?" Jason asked.

Allan played Bloody Mary in the bathroom first. He shut the door and spun around, chanting for Bloody Mary to appear. When Allan yelped Jason knocked on the bathroom door and asked, "Was it Bloody Mary? Did she scratch you?"

"No, I banged my head on the door," Allan grumbled as he came out nursing a bump on his head.

"You can take a selfie and say the Hand hit you," Jason said.

"Huh?"

"The Hand hits. Bloody Mary scratches," Jason said.

"Maybe she'll scratch you. Give it a go," Allan said.

Jason went in and there were a series of bumps. Allan's mother Alice was alerted by the noises and came into the hallway to investigate. She saw her son with a bruise on his forehead and frowned, "What are you two doing?"

"Playing Bloody Mary."

Jason cried out just then. "Did you see Mary?" Allan asked.

"No, I stubbed my toe on the toilet," Jason said as he hobbled out.

"You two shouldn't hog the bathroom. Other people need it too," Alice said.

"Mom! We need a place that has a mirror!" Allan said.

"Use my makeup mirror under the sink and go outside."

"How's Bloody Mary supposed to scratch us if she's only got a teeny, tiny little mirror to work with?" Jason asked.

"That's her problem!"

"Oh," Jason groaned...

The boys found the makeup mirror and moved outside to the tent. They placed the mirror in the center and circled around it chanting, "Bloody Mary, Bloody Mary." Jason used a twirling dance step he'd seen at powwows. Bloody Mary was unimpressed, even when he danced to the point of almost hurling. Allan cried out EWWW! when Jason made a queasy grunt and forced him to sit down before he got sick.

"I don't think Bloody Mary is coming. She must only come for white people." Allan said.

"Maybe your Mom's makeup mirror was too small for her?"

"We must try it again with a bigger mirror," Allan sighed.

"Well we're two Indian kids outside at night so the Hand oughtta show up."

They ate their supper extra slow, but nothing was happening. "How long do you think we must wait?" Allan asked.

"I don't know—maybe midnight?" Jason shrugged.

"That's past my bedtime!"

"Well the Hand comes for bad Indian kids." Jason said.

"How bad do you have to be to see the Hand? Maybe we should try this on a schoolday? Maybe staying up on the weekend isn't bad enough for it?" Allan said.

"It's so much easier to see ghosts in the horror movies!" Jason groaned.

"That's your problem. You're getting all your info from old black and white movies. You need to see new ones to see what it takes to see a ghost nowadays," Allan said.

It made sense to Jason. "Yeah!"

They kept busy while they waited for the Hand. Jason streamed a black and white zombie war movie on a tablet in the tent.

Allan paused it to admire an especially gory zombie. "Our ancestors must've been wimps if they could only stand a hand and not an entire zombie."

"At least our vampires weren't shiny. They were bloodthirsty skeletons. There's nothing for an emo girl to crush on."

"Let's see what Gary's up to on Instagram," Allan said.

"I thought he didn't want us recording him on Devil's Night?" Jason frowned.

"He's got an Instagram account with an avatar called 'G4S'. He uses it to troll people, and keeps his posts anonymous," Allan said.

Gary kept himself off–screen for most of the vlogs. His already heavily made–up face was covered by a beadwork themed bandanna mask when it was visible.

There was a series of short streaming vids on his stream. An apple tree was toilet papered and some toilet paper was used to make hanging ghosts.

Cherry bombs were placed in jack-o'-lanterns and set off while Gary cackled off–screen.

Someone set up a fake tombstone in their frontyard. Gary dug up the ground next to it. He overturned the tombstone to make it look like a body was interred there and had climbed its way out.

Then there were various windows that got egged and doors got pentagrams sprayed on them.

The vids were uploaded in 15 to 20-minute intervals, "He's been busy."

"The Hand should be slapping him around now," Allan laughed.

"Maybe the Hand thinks it's no longer needed now that we have our own police force to patrol the Rez?" Jason asked.

"Yeah," Allan said with a yawn. He was too tired to counter Jason's claims. They turned off the tablet and went to sleep...

They were both awakened by a loud crash and heavy footsteps. The boys were too scared to look outside when they heard loud thuds outside the tent. Dry leaves crinkled under rapid footsteps.

"Let's get inside the house before they come to the back," Allan said to Jason before they raced to the backdoor and locked it behind them.

Once they were protected by the house's walls they had the courage to look at the source of the disturbance. They ran to the window in the living room that faced the front of the house. There was a full moon that night. They made out a frenetic black shadow moving and swatting at the decorations with a heavy baton. It stomped on them with thick, black boots. "It's some punk messing up our decorations. I'm calling 911!" Jason said.

The punk moved into an area lit by a porch light. Allan held Jason's hand before he could type the numbers on the screen, "Don't! I think that's Gary!"

"Gary! What's he doing?" Jason asked. He banged on the window and shouted out, "You're not supposed to trash your own house on Devil's Night."

Just then a pale gray bat flapped its wings in Gary's face and kept swatting him repeatedly. Gary swung his baton at it. He hit the Halloween decorations instead of the bat when it fluttered out of reach as if to mock him. When his baton made a connection, the bat went to the ground.

Gary lost sight of the bat. He found the stuffed monster glove instead and pounded it with the baton and kicked it with his boots.

The bat came back and landed on Gary's neck and clutched it. Allan gasped when he saw it was a disembodied hand whose flesh was as bloodless and dried out as a mummy's. Jason raced to the frontdoor and threw it open before Allan could stop him.

"Are you nuts?" Allan sputtered.

"Get inside the house. The Hand doesn't like Rez kids being out at night," Jason shouted to Gary.

Gary grabbed the Hand and threw it off his neck, so he could race inside. The Hand pulled on his hair as he ran. Gary shook it off before he entered the house. He got enough time to get passed the doorway before all three of them shut it closed.

Pounding started on the other side of the door, and it took all their strength to hold it intact.

There was the sound of heavy footsteps inside the house, "What's going on?" Alice asked as she came down the stairs from her bedroom.

"I got jumped," Gary said.

"By the Hand," Jason added.

Alice shuddered when she saw sweat had smeared Gary's face makeup. Its colors had run, and the red now looked like it was blood oozing out from fresh cuts.

The door handle kept rattling. "" How long is it going to be like this?" Allan asked.

"The Hand sleeps during the day. Dawn should be its bedtime," Jason said.

Alice went to get her own smartphone and took a picture of the Hand at the doorstep from the bay window. She texted the picture to Jason's Mom. "This thing attacked my oldest boy and has us locked inside the house. What am I supposed to do?"

There was a text within minutes. "Keep all the doors and windows locked and stay inside. I'll call a medicine man to come over there, so I can look after Jason and Allan while you take Gary to the hospital."

Alice grabbed her purse and car keys, "Be ready to leave when help comes." she told Gary.

Gary found an old baseball bat inside the house and clutched it as if it were his security blanket...

Jason's Mom, Wanda, and Totah came over within half an hour. Totah had a braid of tobacco in his hand that he lit and used its smoke to smudge the exterior of the house.

The Hand fell to the ground like a gnarly old log in a flower bed at the front of the house. Totah took out a pinch of the Indian Tobacco from his pants' pocket and threw it on the ground, next to it.

The Hand moved on its fingers like a spider and clutched the tobacco like a pincer with its thumb on its back. They waited until it was out of sight before opening the door. Totah handed Gary and Alice a pinch of tobacco and gave them a braid to put inside the house.

"The Hand is ornery, not evil. Burning tobacco calms it down," Totah said.

IT TURNED OUT THAT Gary had nasty cuts and bruises under his face paint. The police wanted Gary to press charges against his assailant. However, he feared identifying the Hand as his attacker would get him locked up in a loony bin.

"I wish I could press charges. It damaged my smartphone!" Gary groused.

"You're lucky it was only a hand. What would a full Rez zombie have done to you?" Jason said to Gary the next time he saw him.

Gary grunted, but no good comeback came to mind. He settled for carrying a pinch of tobacco on him when he went out at night. This time he was out playing evening lacrosse games for a local team. He couldn't stand to stay in after dark now that he was older. He found taking part as a player or watching as a spectator of "the Creator's Game," was an exception to the Hand's curfew.

Gary's G4S feed changed. He stopped trolling other accounts. His uploads focused on his lacrosse practices, games and winning goals four months later.

Jason and Allan didn't have the courage to stay up late at night for any other reason either.

Colette

THE TOBACCO SAP WAS corrosive and ate into the fabric and stuffing of Colette's boudoir doll body. She wanted to scream in rage, but her mouth was fused shut. Soon she'd be disembodied, and it'd be hard to touch the World of the Living.

Worse yet, she couldn't avenge herself on the one responsible for this indignity. Lady Snapping Turtle was surrounded by potent Indian medicine. She'd dismissed the woman's clan of cornhusk dolls as quaint when she first saw them. Yet Grandmother Moon and her "clan" had overwhelmed her.

Colette's mind replayed her last moments in a loop. Was there anything she could've done differently?

She wasn't one to cross and had carried a gold locket that contained photos of her most notable victims. It hadn't been the first time she'd disciplined a sub-par magic practitioner. Madame Savant was the first one she came across and had crafted this boudoir doll body. Colette had been a Hollywood starlet in the 1920s. Her desire to break into the movies caused her to buy a voodoo luck charm from Madame Savant. She got her first big break thereafter but lost her life when she drove home from a gin joint. She'd meant to celebrate the best day in her life, and it turned into the day of her death.

Her rage gave her the power to haunt the bitch. When Madame Savant used a seance to talk to her Colette told her, "I can't get my money back, so I'll take your blood instead."

"What if I offered you a temple to house your spirit? Would that give you peace?"

She accepted the offer and was channeled into a custom-made boudoir doll. Madam Savant gave her jewels and crystals and taught her how to use them. It was nothing more than another ploy to cheat her by turning her into a servant. Yet there was a certain appeal in becoming a first-rate cursing tool. She learned all she could from Madame Savant. When her lessons ended, she took what she learned to set Madame Savant aflame in her bed. She had too much self-respect to become enslaved to the woman who'd cheated her.

Colette's pride had caused her to turn on many owners or to at least train them to treat her with caution and respect. She had a high turnover because of it and now was on the lookout for a new prospect when Lady Snapping Turtle saw her.

Lady Snapping Turtle had been looking to upgrade her "love medicine." How could rustic cornhusk dolls compete with her? Once upon a time they'd had faces, which were taken away to teach them humility. She'd smirked when Grandmother Moon told her the quaint legend. No wonder their owner sought to expand her repertoire beyond her people's medicine.

Perhaps Colette would've been better off avoiding someone from an alien culture. Lady Snapping Turtle could afford her and her mind had an exotic appeal even if her form was on the homely side.

Most of her past hosts were pretty airheads, and it was easy to implant suggestions into their minds. They tended to be young, but she worked with the occasional 'cougar.' She picked who she worked with and had dismissed the latest offerings at the Dark Arts Boutique.

She was set in a mini-shrine so that her beauty could be admired from every angle.

The customers were drawn to her. They came up to admire her, and she assessed them with cool, clear eyes.

First there'd been a dumpling it'd take too long to mold into a useful vessel. The one lust of the flesh Colette despised was that of gluttony.

Then there'd been a woman who took care of herself. However, she outsourced the job to bad contractors who stuffed her with too much silicone. Working with this woman would be like working with a Barbie doll, and she couldn't stand Barbie!

She dismissed every woman who came to the shrine as a suitable host. In her boredom she admired herself in a doll-size mirror.

Seeing herself looking so radiant sweetened her mood. None of these wannabes were in her league, but she could be generous. Let them look, but not touch. Handling her was a privilege for the highest bidder. Most of the shop's participants couldn't afford her.

She wore actual diamonds studs, the only friends she needed, in her ears, around her neck and on a bangle at her wrist. They would've been gaudy bling if they were life-size. However, she approved of the full carets used in her jewelry.

The rest of her was scaled in proportions that flesh and blood women wished they had. Her face modeling was exquisite. She had red cupid's bow lips, sultry eyes with cat's eyes eyeliner, a pert nose in the air and a proud tilt in her chin.

A shadow fell over her, and she came face to face with a broad-faced woman with brown skin and dark hair and eyes. Her jewelry was a "snapping turtle caught in mid-bite" silver pendant. Ostentatious for bling, but worn as if it were a badge of honor instead of an ornament.

She wasn't fat, but built on sturdy lines unlike Colette's long and lean flapper's body. Colette eyes flashed with repressed mirth at the woman's expense. This woman was a cow not a cougar, and she was too heartless to pity such an Unfortunate.

The woman's eyes narrowed as if reading her mind. Colette's heart would've skipped a beat if she had one anymore. The woman gave a knowing smirk delighting in her discomfiture.

The woman turned and Colette watched her go to the boutique's owner, Sister Delilah, "How much is that boudoir doll?"

Her voice reverberated in Colette's body with power and authority. She recognized it as a voice of command despite herself. The knowing smirk of her painted lips deepened. *Ah, I know what you are now. Not, a maiden, mother nor crone. You are a wisewoman.* Wisewomen were often of middle years, past the age of vanity but without the frailties of old age. Most men thought the height of a women's beauty was the pinnacle of women's power. They didn't know wisewomen commanded the most power among female practitioners of magic.

She didn't understand who this woman was, but she welcomed the challenge, *Either you'll dominate me or I'll crush you. You'll make a hard master or a worthy conquest. Either of which will amuse me.*

"Colette's price is $6660," Sister Delilah said.

"I must know the doll's provenance before I pay that kind of money," the woman said.

Either you're wise or you're cheap. Colette sighed. She adjusted her hopes to cautious optimism. She'd seen her best hosts make sharp deals before. Though there were times a bargain hunter was nothing more than a cheese parer.

"If you take Colette, Lady Snapping Turtle, it must be to a forever home:

Colette, the Femme Fatale, was commissioned from Madame Savant. She was one of the top enchantresses in her day. Her clients were told her products would give 'IT' to them.

Lady Snapping Turtle nodded, "She sounds like she'd be good for love medicine."

The woman handed over a "tax card" before the order was rung in. She could afford Colette's price and had certain privileges. *What are you, Lady Snapping Turtle?* Colette wondered.

WHEN THEY WERE ALONE in Lady Snapping Turtle's hotel room Colette's box was opened. A lace sachet was placed next to Colette.

Colette sniffed, *Really lavender?* Her estimation of the woman fell. Yet her disdain turned to wonder when she recognized the scent. She's so enthralled by me, she's making me offerings of fresh tobacco?

Most times she waited until her thralls were broken before she could receive such homage. Her thoughts were so happy she didn't notice when the lid was put back into the box. The darkness and tobacco aroma were a delightful cocoon she didn't want to leave. It was more seductive than the Chanel No. 5 she had her thralls spritz on her in the later stages of their enchantment.

Her gloating gave her a buzz that made her time in the box pass by in a blur which ended when the box was reopened. She found herself in a large log home instead of a hotel room. *That tobacco must've been bespelled if I didn't even notice time passing! I'm in the hands of a true mistress of magic!*

It was now nighttime. She was in a room full of beadwork designed cloth furnishings. This woman had money but her aesthetics and priorities differed from Colette's.

Lady Snapping Turtle turned on Bluetooth speakers. Drum music instead of the smooth jazz Colette preferred played. At least it had an organic sound like a beating heart and wasn't a rock'n roll bass rhythm. It was odd though not too jarring to Colette.

She saw a wall full of niches. Each niche housed a cornhusk doll, some of whom shifted at the sight of her, *Are they all animated by spirits? Lady Snapping*

Turtle must be powerful if she could capture so many spirits to serve her. Colette counted the dolls in the collection to see how many lost souls Lady Snapping Turtle ensnared. Colette saw they were cornhusk dolls who looked no better than rustic scarecrows. Their faces were blank. They wore calico and ribbon dresses and black and dark blue broadcloth leggings. She tilted her head to make her diamond studs flash. To show she had proper jewelry not beadwork to adorn her, *Lady Snapping Turtle is ready to trade up.*

"I need to smudge you," Lady Snapping Turtle said.

Smudge. She will smudge my makeup! Colette's eyes widened in alarm.

Lady Snapping Turtle took down an eagle feather fan with a black beaded handle from a niche in the wall. She took a packet of tobacco and a bowl carved from what looked like cheap gray marble to Colette. She placed a plug of tobacco in the bowl. Took out a sliver lighter and let the plug. A lid with a smoke hole on top was put on the bowl.

You use tobacco as incense? I need to educate you.

She assumed the tobacco was used as an air freshener. To her outrage the eagle fan was used to waft the smoke over her, *How dare you blow smoke in my face!* Colette tried to say, but the words stuck in her throat as if the smoke glued her mouth shut. She could only grunt.

The indignity kept going on and on. The smoke was wafted over every inch of her body from front to back. Colette could only fume in rage. *Outrageous!*

She'd disciplined other owners for less than this.

When it was done Lady Snapping Turtle blew out the smoldering tobacco and retired for the night. Yet Colette wasn't able to spring into action. The cornhusk dolls moved from their spots on the shelves and swarmed around her in a circle.

"Sago, I am Grandmother Moon. This is my clan." the largest doll said. It had a dried apple face and hands that looked like elderly human flesh, and white yarn as her hair. She motioned to the other cornhusk dolls when she mentioned the word "clan."

"Huh? Sago?"

"It means 'hello' in Mohawk," Grandmother Moon said.

"Oh, I only know English and Latin," Colette said, thinking it best to be polite to the spokesperson of the swarm.

Colette noticed the beadwork on their bodies was ball pins inserted into them. One unfortunate had a vice grip screwed on its head. She stared at it too long, and it said, "I'm helping Snapping Turtle give her greatest critic migraines."

"Oh–doesn't that leave a mark?" Colette didn't feel pain herself but didn't like rough play. Otherwise, she wouldn't have pushed that one spoiled brat down a set of stairs.

"Yes, but it's for a good cause," Vice Grip said.

"I'm sure Lady Snapping Turtle appreciates what you do for her," Colette said. She was sure she'd never have to endure such an indignity. Vice Grip was made of simple materials and cheap cloth. He wasn't as big an investment as she was.

She had to keep up the conversation lest this mob suspect her condescension. "I hope she makes it worth your while?".

"We get regular tobacco burnings and a yearly feast," Grandmother Moon said.

"A feast?"

"Traditional food is left out as a dedication to us, and we get to savor its essence," Grandmother Moon said.

"I come from the Roaring 20s. I prefer cigarettes and bathtub gin myself," Colette couldn't stop herself from sniffing.

"Alcohol destroys our medicine. Gin would be an insult to us."

"It must frustrate you all to have such a counterspell," Colette cooed.

"Yeah, but we can turn it against them. Snapping Turtle once had a rival who knew of the counter. We got what we wanted by keeping at her until her liver got wrecked," Grandmother Moon cackled.

"Hm, I know Lady Snapping Turtle isn't a white witch, but I'm surprised to hear such a story from you?"

"I am named after the Creator's grandmother. He has an evil twin she prefers even though she raised them both. She keeps her favorite grandson company on the darkside," Grandmother Moon said.

"It never occurred to me that a woman would still prefer the bad boys even if she was a crone," Colette said.

Grandmother Moon cackled at this. "I never thought of it that way, but we understand each other."

She motioned to another cornhusk doll. It carried a mollusk shell with iridescent purple and white insides as a serving platter. There were beads carved of the same type of shell inside it. Grandmother Moon chose a string of white beads and gave it to Colette, "This is white wampum. It symbolizes peace."

Then she pointed to the dark purple beads, "Black wampum means war and death among my clan."

Colette took the bead string and placed it in her sequined clutch purse accessory. She would've preferred black pearls, but thought it best not to mock the symbolism of the act.

"You are now one of us."

The introduction would've ended on a high note if it'd ended there. Things changed when the mob dispersed to carry out their chores. Two girl dolls went to a hollow stump, put dried white corn kernels into it and pounded them into a powder. Others swept and used cloths to clean the room.

"Huh," Colette asked when Grandmother Moon gestured to a feather duster, "Now you can do the dusting."

"I'm a tool of enchantment, not a cleaning appliance," Colette sputtered.

"The first cornhusk doll was a beauty like you. She spent days admiring herself in pools instead of doing what the Creator assigned her to do. She got warnings but ignored them. Until the day came when the Creator took away her face, so it could no longer distract her," Grandmother Moon said.

Colette snapped, "It'll take more than one of your people's fables to scare me."

"Then consider this: there are times Snapping Turtle wishes to curse one of her enemies until they die. When that happens a cornhusk doll is covered with an acidic potion and buried and left to rot in a mini-coffin. Most times we create a mindless effigy for that ourselves. Sometimes we volunteer one of our own for that. Someone who hasn't been making contributions."

Colette sniffed and pointed her nose into the air, "You wouldn't dare! I cost Lady Snapping Turtle more than your entire clan. I'm not some cheap, throwaway piece of scrap. She values me more than she values any of you."

The cornhusk dolls muttered at this. Some stepped forward, but Grandmother Moon held up her hand. She spoke, "Snapping Turtle values her life more than she values money. She knows we'll turn on her if she won't allow us to keep you in line."

Colette ground her inset teeth. Though she accepted the feather duster Grandmother Moon gave her.

Colette's teeth kept grinding as she did the work assigned to her. The rest of the dolls dispersed to their chores. A carpenter doll made a point of constructing a doll coffin as she muttered, *They will all pay for this*, to herself.

AT LEAST COLETTE WAS right about having a higher market value than the cornhusk dolls. Lady Snapping Turtle proved it the next morning. "Get ready for an inspection. My insurance broker says you need to get appraised tomorrow."

Colette smirked at this. Let the other dolls think it was only vanity, but she saw this as the perfect opportunity to avenge herself.

No one found it strange when she took out her crystal ball to charge in the sun. She smiled as she polished the crystal with a black silk cloth. *Soon, soon.*

"It's a pretty trinket but is too small for Lady Snapping Turtle to use," Grandmother Moon commented.

Colette couldn't help but caress the crystal ball, *It's mine, not Lady Snapping Turtle's.*

Hosts needed discipline occasionally. She would hold Lady Snapping Turtle responsible for the indignities she'd endured.

COLETTE'S DEPARTURE reminded her why she wanted to leave this band of savages yet again. Lady Snapping Turtle checked to see if she'd packed everything in her wardrobe. Colette lay prone in her box when Grandmother Moon loomed over her with a satchel full of tobacco. She couldn't help scowling despite that fetching fragrance.

"Take this with you," Grandmother Moon said to Lady Snapping Turtle.

Lady Snapping Turtle waved it away. "The appraiser will lower Colette's value if they know I'll expose her to tobacco smoke. I can't let them see it near Colette."

Grandmother Moon grunted and whispered to Colette. "Things will be different once the insurance gives you a replacement value. Humans get killed for insurance payouts and dolls are easier to replace."

Colette raised up a hand to swat Grandmother Moon away, but the matron avoided the slap with a chuckle.

I must get out of here before I'm put on Lady Snapping Turtle's insurance rider.

COLETTE WAS PLACED in the backseat of the car. Her wardrobe was openable from the inside, so she freed herself when the car was moving. She checked to make sure Lady Snapping Turtle's attention was focused on the road first.

She then took out her crystal ball from its black velvet pouch.

Colette jumped when Lady Snapping Turtle asked, "what do you think you're doing?" from the driver's seat.

She groaned to see that her crystal ball was generating rainbows once it was out in the light, "Stop that!"

Colette panicked when she felt them swerve to the side of the road and set off the flash. The car rolled over on its side locking Colette inside with Lady Snapping Turtle.

"Our sensors have picked up an abrupt turn. Do you require assistance?" a voice boomed over the cars' speaker.

Colette ground her teeth, Damn modern day road side assistance. She never had to deal with this back in the day!

"We are calling 911, and your emergency contact Grandmother Moon."

"No!" Colette cried out.

OF COURSE, THE RESCUE crew only cared about Lady Snapping Turtle when they came. Colette hid while they cleared the path for her while they got the human out. A smell of burnt tobacco in the air made Colette shudder when she emerged from the wreck. Two warrior cornhusk dolls took hold of Colette by the arms.

"Let me go, you savages," she cried out.

They carried her to the ground. Grandmother Moon awaited with a string of dark purple wampum beads on her arm. Grandmother Moon gestured to the wreckage. "As a Clanmother I can declare this an act of war."

She placed the beads around Colette's neck as if it was a garland, and removed her diamond jewelry, "No!"

She squirmed as they carried her to a doll coffin. There was a pit dug next to it and a birchbark container.

Colette's captors laid her flat in the coffin. Another pair of warriors took out T-pins and pinned her tight to its lining. Grandmother Moon took up the birchbark container, "Tobacco plant sap is corrosive. It's part of the potion we place on a doll meant to represent a person Snapping Turtle wishes dead. Now you're the one we want cursed."

Colette screamed as the sap was poured over her body until it went over her head and her cries became gurgles. Grandmother Moon nodded. The lid was placed on the top of the coffin and then nail studs got pounded into its rim.

They lowered the coffin into the ground. All Colette could do was squirm and squeal in her world of darkness.

I'm the product of black magic. This can't be happening to me.

There were dull thuds as clods of dirt fell onto the coffin until the final awful moment when they stopped.

The corrosive sap etched her humiliation in her mind, leaving her forever alone with her rage.

About the Author

CATHY SMITH IS A MOHAWK writer who lives on a Status Reservation on the Canadian Side of the Border.

She is proud of her people's heritage, and has an interest in the traditions of other cultures. Most of her works to date have been based on the folkloric traditions she's studied. Science fiction and fantasy strikes her as the folklore of the modern age and she considers both genres a natural choice for her own writings.

You can also follow her at:

Twitter: @khiatons

Facebook: bit.ly/2dP3rXd

Wordpress: bit.ly/2e41qWT

Pinterest: bit.ly/2fGMgqP

Instagram: cathy2891

Tumblr: bit.ly/2G3dEjo

Sign up to the Cathy Smith-Khiatons-I Write Substack https://bit.ly/4qATMGH to receive news and excerpts of new publications and promotions.

www.ingramcontent.com/pod-product-compliance
Lightning Source LLC
Chambersburg PA
CBHW051830130726
47987CB00003B/1488